CONGRATULATIONS, MISS MALARKEY!

Judy Finchler
&
Kevin O'Malley

Illustrations by
Kevin O'Malley

WALKER & COMPANY ✸ NEW YORK

E
FIN

First published in the United States of America in 2009 by Walker Publishing Company, Inc.
Visit Walker & Company's Web site at www.walkeryoungreaders.com

For information about permission to reproduce selections from this book, write to
Permissions, Walker & Company, 175 Fifth Avenue, New York, New York 10010

Library of Congress Cataloging-in-Publication Data
Finchler, Judy.
Congratulations, Miss Malarkey! / Judy Finchler and Kevin O'Malley ; illustrations by Kevin O'Malley.
p.   cm.
Summary: Miss Malarkey is behaving very strangely, giggling in the halls and teaching lessons about marriage
customs, as her students worry that she is quitting teaching.
ISBN-13: 978-0-8027-9835-0 • ISBN-10: 0-8027-9835-7 (hardcover)
ISBN-13: 978-0-8027-9836-7 • ISBN-10: 0-8027-9836-5 (reinforced)
[1. Teachers—Fiction. 2. Schools—Fiction. 3. Marriage—Fiction.] I. O'Malley, Kevin, ill. II. Title.
PZ7.F495666Con 2009   [E]—dc22   2008035041

Art created with markers and colored pencils
Typeset in Charlotte Book

Printed in China by C&C Offset Printing Co. LTD.
2 4 6 8 10 9 7 5 3 1 (hardcover)
2 4 6 8 10 9 7 5 3 1 (reinforced)

All papers used by Walker & Company are natural, recyclable products
made from wood grown in well-managed forests. The manufacturing processes
conform to the environmental regulations of the country of origin.

Just as family provides us roots, best friends bring beautiful flowers: to my best friends, Ellen & Lenny, Arlene & Irwin, and, of course, Sue —J. F.

Miss Malarkey has been acting really strange lately.

She giggles a lot when she walks down the hall.

She sings to herself.

Her teacher friends keep stopping her in the hall and giggling with her.

I even saw Principal Wiggins laugh so hard with her in his office that his hair almost slipped off.

I asked my friend Jonathan what he thought was going on.

"Maybe she won a lot of money," he said.

"I think she's going to be in a movie or on TV," said Louise.

"Maybe she's going to become an astronaut and fly to Mars," said Paul as he looked up from the book he was reading.

Everybody agreed she wasn't going to Mars.

"I heard Principal Wiggins say something about quitting teaching," said Raul.

"No way. Miss Malarkey is the greatest. She wouldn't quit," I said, but I was worried.

Miss Malarkey is the best teacher I've ever had. And I've had five whole teachers.

She taught me about books and how to stay calm during a test. She even taught me how to kick a ball really far during recess.

Miss Malarkey wouldn't
quit teaching. Would she?

So I worried. I worried for days and days.

On the playground I forgot how to kick the ball.

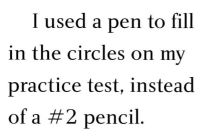

I used a pen to fill in the circles on my practice test, instead of a #2 pencil.

And when I read a book, I kept losing my place because my brain kept picturing one of our strange substitutes taking over for Miss Malarkey.

Then Miss Malarkey started teaching us really boring stuff. In world cultures we started a unit about weddings.

"Some brides will take their husband's last name. Your art teacher was called Miss Zelinsky before she got married. Now you call her Mrs. Sykes. Mrs. Downing-Rodgers uses both her husband's last name and her own last name."

The girls in the class really got into it. So did some of the boys, but most of us just thought it was weird.

COOL!

We learned about Jewish people, who stand under a chuppah when they get married by a person called a rabbi. All the men wear a yarmulke on their heads, and when the ceremony is done the guy smashes a glass that's covered with a napkin.

In Mexico, the guy gives the girl thirteen gold coins to show how much he loves her. The guests form a heart-shaped circle around the couple as they dance.

YUCK!

In Puerto Rico, a doll that looks like the bride is covered with little good-luck charms and placed at the head of the table. The bride and groom give the guests a ribbon thing to thank them for showing up.

DOUBLE YUCK!

In Egypt, just before the couple says "I do," they march in a wedding dance called the Zaffa. There are belly dancers and horns and drums and guys with flaming swords.

AWESOME!

All right, some of the wedding stuff was kind of cool. But I couldn't stop worrying about Miss Malarkey quitting teaching. Now she was singing out loud in the halls.

I couldn't take it anymore. So I stayed behind after school one day and waited for Miss Malarkey to come outside.

"You're going to quit teaching, aren't you?
I knew it! You can't quit teaching! You can't!" I
realized I was yelling and my face had turned red.

"Relax," said Miss Malarkey. "I'm not going anywhere. I've been keeping a secret from you kids, but tomorrow you'll find out what it is."

I felt better, but that night I had trouble sleeping. Maybe she really was going to be an astronaut. I dreamed about Martians all night.

The next morning, Miss Malarkey handed every kid in the class an envelope. We all opened them at the same time.

It was a wedding invitation!

Miss Malarkey was getting married, and she was inviting the whole class to come to the church and watch!

The wedding was only days away, on Saturday.

When Saturday came, my mom said I had to look nice for the wedding, so I put on my best pair of shorts and a clean T-shirt. I even put on clean socks.

Mom made me put on a button-down shirt. Then my dad tied a tie for me.

A lot of my friends went to the wedding. The church was crowded with people. I saw a lot of teachers from our school. I didn't even recognize Mr. Buffup, the custodian. He looked like a millionaire!

The wedding started, and Principal Wiggins was holding Miss Malarkey's arm as they walked into the church. It looked like Miss Malarkey should have been holding *his* arm instead. His legs didn't seem to work very well.

The guy Miss Malarkey was gonna marry had a big chin.

The priest talked for a while. The church started getting hot, but nobody in my class caused any trouble. Finally Miss Malarkey said, "I do." Everybody clapped and cheered.

On the way out of the church, we all lined up and blew bubbles at the bride and groom as they got into a sweet limo. A lot of people laughed. Some people cried, but they were smiling.

I was just glad Miss Malarkey wasn't quitting teaching.

Miss Malarkey was out of school for a while on her honeymoon. We had a substitute who painted her nails while we did worksheets.

I got to thinking about Miss Malarkey's new last name. She married a man named Bob Fulla. Were we going to have to call her Mrs. Fulla now?

I waited outside school on the morning Miss Malarkey was coming back. When her car pulled up, I ran over.

"Miss Malarkey, Miss Malarkey," I said, "what are we supposed to call you now? Should we call you Mrs. Fulla-Malarkey?"

Miss Malarkey put her hand on my shoulder. "No," she said, and she laughed really hard. "You can just call me *Mrs. Malarkey*."